The Wishing Tree

by Roseanne Thong

illustrated by Connie McLennan

SHEN'S
BOOKS

Book design by Laurel Ann Mathe, Mystic Design, Inc. ◆ Colfax, California

Sharing a World of Stories
40951 Fremont Blvd.
Fremont, CA 94538
Toll Free 800-456-6660
www.shens.com
info@shens.com

SHEN'S
BOOKS

Printed in Hong Kong

10   9 8 7 6 5 4 3 2 1

Library of Congress Cataloging-in-Publication Data

Thong, Roseanne.
The wishing tree / by Roseanne Thong ; illustrated by Connie McLennan.
        p. cm.
Summary: At the wishing tree on Lunar New Year with his grandmother Ming's wishes always
seemed to come true, but one year the tree does not help, and he alone must make peace with the
loss of his grandmother and the spirit of the tree.
    ISBN 1-885008-26-0
    [1. Chinese New Year--Folklore--Fiction. 2. Grief--Fiction. 3. Death--Fiction.
4. Grandmothers--Fiction. 5. Wishes--Fiction.] I. McLennan, Connie, ill. II. Title.
PZ7.T3815Wi 2004
[E]--dc22   2004011950

To Maya,
hoping that all your wishes and dreams come true,
to the Hong Kong SCBWI for your advice and support,
and to Pion, Ruby, and Wei for your Chinese expertise!
~ R. T.

For Thomas.
~ C.M.

An enormous banyan tree with thick, leafy branches grew in the center of a village near an ancient temple in a green valley with a gurgling stream.

The tree had been there for as long as Ming's grandmother could remember, and certainly much longer than that. Winter, spring, summer and fall, it was covered with thousands of wishes. Each wish was written on brightly-colored paper, tied on with string, and weighted with a large Mandarin orange. People came from near and far to toss their requests and desires into its sturdy branches.

When Ming was five years old,
Grandmother took him to make
his first wish. It was Lunar New
Year, and the tree's enormous canopy
of leaves glistened with red and gold.
Ming was spellbound by the sight.

"The tree is generous with its
magic," Grandmother explained.
"Villagers say that long ago it helped
a boy make incredible improvements
in his studies. They also say it led a
rich stranger to the village, who paid
for the temple's construction."

Ming was filled with excitement and couldn't wait to make a wish. There were many vendors selling paper and string, but Grandmother led him to a cheerful, moon-faced woman whom she knew well. "This is my grandson," she said. "He's come to make his first wish."

Smiling, the vendor pulled out a crisp bundle of paper and handed it to Ming. "Wish carefully," Grandmother advised, "but remember that even wishing trees have their limitations."

又高又壯
big and strong

After Ming finished writing, Grandmother showed him how to roll up the wish like a scroll and hurl it skyward into the tree's outstretched arms. The first time, Ming didn't throw his bundle hard enough and it fell back down to earth with a heavy thud. He tried five more times before he was successful. After all, it was a huge tree, and he was just a small boy.

Ming's wish was to be tall and strong like his older brother. All year long he thought about the wish and anxiously waited to see if it would be granted. Sure enough, by the following year he had grown a foot taller and was strong enough to help move the heavy chairs in his parents' restaurant.

熱鬧
exciting

Convinced of the tree's magic, the next year
Ming wished for something exciting to happen
in the village. A few months later, a movie crew
came to make a kung fu film. The movie starred
several famous actors, and Ming and his friends
were allowed to watch them perform. Even better,
they got to collect the actors' autographs.

不受欺負
no bullying

As the years passed, Ming came to depend on the tree. It was like a member of his family who always helped him out.

One year, Ming faced a difficult problem. A boy from another village moved to his school and began bullying him. The new boy was taller and stronger than everyone else. Although Ming tried to stay away, the bully followed him home and demanded money and sweets. Ming's wish that year was to be rid of the bully forever. To his surprise, his father bought a new restaurant in the city, and a few months later, the family moved away from the village.

Although their new home was far from the Wishing Tree, Ming and Grandmother still went to visit each year. They would board a bus early in the morning and carry a picnic lunch to eat under the tree's wide, leafy branches. All afternoon, they would watch other wish-makers toss their requests skyward, and would stay until the last rays of light faded from behind the temple eaves.

When Ming was nine, Grandmother became very sick and could no longer get out of bed. Ming visited the Wishing Tree alone that year and asked it to cure Grandmother's illness. He wrote his request on the shiniest red paper he could find, and used the most polite and sincere language he knew.

When he threw the wish into the air, it immediately caught hold on a strong, thick branch where the wind could not blow it off. Ming thought this was a good sign, and went home with a smile on his face. After all, the tree had always granted his wishes before.

But this time, the magic didn't work. Grandmother died soon afterwards and Ming felt sad and bitter. He missed grandmother's gentle laugh and the stories she had shared with him. He also felt betrayed by the tree. He had visited it so many times—how could it have let him down? Ming swore he would never return to the Wishing Tree again.

Several years passed and Ming forced
the tree out of his mind. Then, one
Lunar New Year, an old schoolmate
named Hong invited him back to the
village for a class reunion. Ming's
thoughts flooded with sad memories.
Still, his friends wanted him to join
them, so he agreed.

As soon as Ming got off the bus, he realized how much he missed the peaceful, green valley where he had grown up. On the way to Hong's house, he stopped by the ancient temple and leapt across the gurgling stream where he had played as a child.

After a delicious lunch with his friends, the boys walked over to the Wishing Tree. It was more beautiful than Ming had remembered it.

While the other boys made wishes, Ming and Hong took a seat and chatted about old times. But when the sky turned orange and the sun slipped behind the mountains' hunchbacked slopes, a tear slipped down Ming's cheek. He told Hong how much he missed his grandmother, and how they used to make wishes together.

"What did she wish for the last time you were here?" asked Hong.

"Grandmother always wished for the same thing," Ming said, "for my happiness."

"And are you happy?"

Ming thought about the question for a long time.
He liked his new school and had made many new
friends. He was taking kung fu lessons and was one
of the best in the class. In fact, he had just won first
place at a local competition. The trophy was shiny and
gold, and he smiled whenever he saw it on his shelf.
Ming realized that the Wishing Tree *had* granted his
grandmother's last wish. Suddenly, his anger left, and
he forgave the tree the way one forgives a good friend
after an argument.

Ming ran over to a familiar vendor who was just
packing up her wares for the night. "Please sell me a
piece of paper," he begged. "I won't have another
chance to make a wish until next year."

At first the vendor said no, but then she recognized Ming as the boy she knew many years before. She smiled, unpacked her nearly-empty box, and took out her last piece of wrinkled, red wishing paper. Ming scribbled down his message as quickly as he could and tossed it high into the branches. He concentrated hard and mumbled several words as he threw. He was taller now, and his wish lodged snuggly on a large branch on his first try.

"What did you wish for?" asked Hong.

"Not for a single thing," Ming replied.

Hong looked puzzled. He had clearly seen Ming write something down on the paper just minutes before. Then Ming explained.

"In all the years that I've come to the
tree, I've never shown my appreciation.
This time I didn't ask for anything—
I said thank you instead."

Author's Note

This story is based on a local legend about a real tree in the village of Lam Tsuen in Hong Kong. According to the legend, Lam Tsuen really did have a slow learner who improved in his studies, as well as a rich visitor who paid for the temple to be built.

Although Lam Tsuen has the most famous Wishing Tree in Hong Kong, is not the only one. The Hong Kong countryside is dotted with smaller, lesser-known wishing trees. Wishing trees tend to be banyan or camphor trees—probably because these varieties have large aerial roots that twist and curve into strange and unusual shapes. It is easy to imagine that these amazing roots have special powers.

In ancient times, people assigned each child to a particular tree, which was supposed to protect (or watch over) the child. When the child was sick or if exam pressures were high, special offerings of fruit, red candles, or wine would be made to the spirit of the tree.

Today, people visit the Wishing Tree to make all types of wishes. They come throughout the year, but it is especially crowded during Lunar New Year and on the 1st and 15th of each month, which are traditional Chinese days of worship.

Visitors purchase five-layered bundles of paper called *Ng Bo Dip*, or Five Treasure Piles, to write their wishes on. The papers are red and gold in color, signifying good luck. After the wishes are written, they are rolled into scrolls and tied to oranges with string. The weight of the oranges makes the bundles easier to throw, and causes the string to tangle in the tree's branches. This way, the wind cannot blow them away.

Like Ming in the story, children from all over Hong Kong, as well as visitors from all over the world, come to cast their wishes, hopes, and dreams into the Wishing Tree's wide, leafy branches. And who knows- their wishes just might come true!

Make a Wish with your own *Ng Bo Dip!*

Ng Bo Dip means "Five Treasures Pile" in Cantonese.
It is made of five sheets of lucky red and yellow paper,
all rolled up into a scroll. People write wishes on them
and toss them into the branches of Wishing Trees.
It's easy to make your own *Ng Bo Dip.*

You will need:

- 1-5 sheets of paper
- A piece of tape
- A three-foot-long piece of string or ribbon
- A pencil or pen
- One large orange
- A stapler

1. Photocopy the wishing paper on the opposite page, or draw your own with lucky colors and designs. You can use up to five sheets of paper.

2. Write your wish in the center of the paper and roll it up. If you used more than one sheet, roll them up together. Use some tape to keep the scroll from unrolling.

3. Tie one end of the ribbon or string around a large orange. You may want to use the stapler to help make it stay.

4. Tie the other end of your ribbon or string tightly around your paper scroll.

5. Now you're ready to make a wish. Throw your *Ng Bo Dip* into a tree. *If it catches on a branch, perhaps your wish will come true!*